To my parents Lucinda Jackson and Mark Tanks (RIH) who encouraged every dream and gave me the gift of writing. ~ ZTJ

Meet AMINA,
she loves
school,
loves to add,
and read.

AMINA loves
her brother and
sister, and
eating fresh
veggies.

All these things bring **AMINA** a smile, happiness, and joy.

The BOOM BOOM, roar from the sky, always have her hiding under the sheets.

The flash from the lightning, SPLIZZ, SPLAZZ, have her heart skipping beats.

Sometimes the thunder and lightning, keeps AMINA awake; tumbling throughout the night, wondering, "Can I catch a break?".

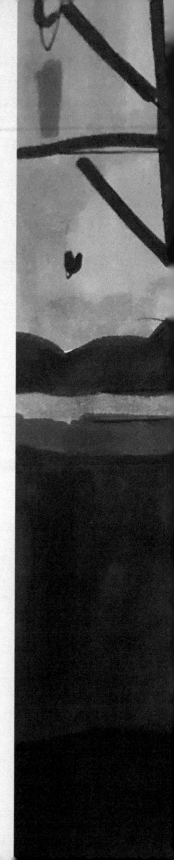

One day, AMINA, asked Bigma, "How can I stop storms?"

"O dear, they are part of nature's beauty; water for grass and streams. The sounds are sweet music that helps us drift to calm dreams."

Bigma sat beside AMINA'S bed and began to hum a tune, to help her precious granddaughter peacefully sleep under the moon.

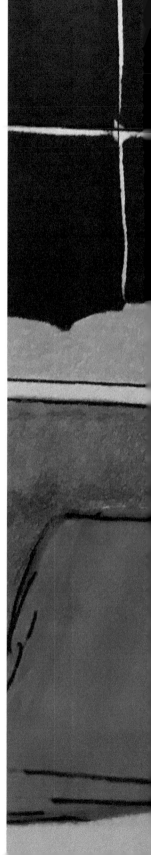

"Thunder and
lightning you've
come to town
today, bringing
fruitful gifts of
water and music
for the trees
and flowers to
sway."

"BOOM-BOOM, Splitzz Splatzz, SWOOSH, I hear the wind; swirling around, up and down, BOOM, there's thunder again."

"SPLITZZ SPLATZZ, flash flash, looks like a camera to me. Click click, SPLAZZ. What an awesome image to see!"

"O, my, what a busy storm tonight, dancing the night away. I thank GOD I'm able to see and hear his wonderful theatrical play."

AMINA was sound asleep and as Bigma rose to kiss her cheek....

BOOM BOOM, Splitzz Splatzz, SWOOSH there's the wind, softly soothing everyones dreams and will soon come to an end.

CPSIA information can be obtained
at www.ICGtesting.com
Printed in the USA
LVHW020100270520
656402LV00007B/561

9 781714 387540